Twelve Plump Cookies

Written by Larry Dane Brimner • Illustrated by Sharon Holm

JE Brimner

Published in the United States of America by The Child's World®
PO Box 326 • Chanhassen, MN 55317-0326
800-599-READ • www.childsworld.com

Reading Adviser

Cecilia Minden-Cupp, PhD, Director of Language and Literacy, Harvard University Graduate School of Education, Cambridge, Massachusetts

Acknowledgments

The Child's World®: Mary Berendes, Publishing Director

Editorial Directions, Inc.: E. Russell Primm, Editorial Director and Project Manager; Katie Marsico, Associate Editor; Judith Shiffer, Assistant Editor; Matt Messbarger, Editorial Assistant

The Design Lab: Kathleen Petelinsek, Design and Art Production

Library of Congress Cataloging-in-Publication Data

Brimner, Larry Dane.
  Twelve plump cookies / written by Larry Dane Brimner ; illustrated by Sharon Holm.
    p. cm. — (Magic door to learning)
  Summary: Egbert practices division as he shares cookies with his friends and neighbors.
  ISBN 1-59296-523-7 (library bound : alk. paper) [1. Division—Fiction. 2. Mathematics—Fiction.
3. Sharing—Fiction. 4. Cookies—Fiction.] I. Holm, Sharon Lane, ill. II. Title.
  PZ7.B767Twe 2005
  [E]—dc22   2005005374

A book is a door, a magic door.
It can take you places
you have never been before.
Ready? Set?
Turn the page.
Open the door.
Now it is time to explore.

One Saturday Egbert made cookies—
twelve plump cookies just ready to eat!
Knock. Knock.

It was Egbert's friend Louise.
"Would you like some cookies?" Egbert asked.

"Yes, please!" said Louise.

Egbert got two plates. He started counting, "One for you, and one for me."

Pretty soon the two plates were full. How many cookies were ready to eat?

Six plump cookies would make
a fine, fine treat. But . . .
Knock! Knock!

Knock!
Knock!

9

It was Señor Lopez and his son Ricky.

"Would you like some cookies?" Egbert asked.

"Sí," said Señor Lopez. "Gracias."

Egbert got two more plates and started counting again. How many cookies were ready to eat?

Three plump cookies would make a fine, fine treat. But . . . *Knock! Knock!*

13

It was Uncle Nick and
Aunt Rosa.

"Would you like some
cookies?" Egbert asked
them.

"Well, of course."

How many cookies were
stacked, ready to eat?

Two plump cookies would make a fine, fine treat. But . . . *Knock! Knock!*

17

"I smelled something wonderful," said Mr. Zing, the neighbor.

"I just made some cookies," said Egbert. "Would you like some?"

Mr. Zing marched in. Mrs. Zing and the four little Zings marched in behind him.

Egbert took out six more plates. How many cookies were stacked, ready to eat?

One plump cookie still would make a fine treat. But . . . Knock! Knock!

knock
knock

21

"Would you like some
cookies?" Grandpa
asked. "Grandma and
I just made them."
    And everyone had
a fine, fine treat.

Our story is over, but there is still much to explore beyond the magic door!

Do you like chocolate chip cookies? Ask an adult to help you bake a batch, and be prepared to share! Count the number of people you plan to share with. How many cookies should each person get? Be sure that everyone receives an equal amount!

These books will help you explore at the library and at home:

Lewis, Paeonv, and Brita Granström. *No More Cookies!* New York: Chicken House/Scholastic, 2005.

Numberoff, Laura Joffe, and Felicia Bond (illustrator). *If You Give a Mouse a Cookie.* New York: Harper & Row, 1985.

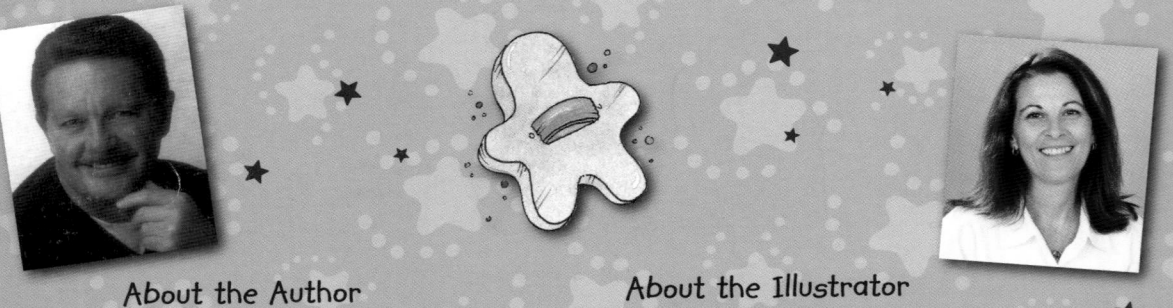

About the Author

Larry Dane Brimner is an award-winning author of more than 120 books for children. When he isn't at his computer writing, he can be found biking in Colorado or hiking in Arizona. You can visit him online at *www.brimner.com*.

About the Illustrator

Sharon Lane Holm is a resident of New Fairfield, Conn. She lives with her husband and son, one dog, three cats, two birds, and fish. Holm has illustrated many educational readers, picture books, and children's craft books. *Zoe's Hats*, a color concept book that Sharon wrote as well as illustrated, was published in 2003.